TRUTH SERUM PRESS

WISER

truth serum vol. 2

First published September 2017

Truth Serum Press
4 Warburton Street
Magill SA 5072
Australia

Email: truthserumpress@live.com.au
Website: http://truthserumpress.net
Truth Serum Press catalogue: http://truthserumpress.net/catalogue/

Original front cover artwork by Damasque Wells
Cover design by Matt Potter

ISBN: 978-1-925536-31-7

Also available as an eBook
ISBN: 978-1-925536-32-4

A note on differences in punctuation and spelling

Truth Serum Press proudly features writers from all over the English-speaking world. Some
speak and write English as their first language, while for others, it's their second or third or even
fourth language. Naturally, across all versions of English, there are differences in punctuation
and spelling, and even in meaning. These differences are reflected in the work *Truth Serum
Press* publishes, and it accounts for any differences in punctuation, spelling and meaning found
within these pages.

Contents

Commute / Claudia Bierschenk / 9

Sometimes Electives Aren't / Paul Beckman / 10

Chickens / Len Kuntz / 12

Woefully Wiser / Jan Elman Stout / 15

Dear Students / Martin Jon Porter / 18

Planet Fykaluxt / Allan J. Wills / 20

Rogue Desire / Cynthia Leslie-Bole / 22

Wising Up / Rick Blum / 25

18 Nots / Ron Campbell / 28

Crossing crossings / Piet Nieuwland / 30

Hallowed Halls / Todd McKie / 32

Miss Palmerston's Ring / Nod Ghosh / 36

going dry at the poetry slam / Rob Walker / 40

Wisdom / Matt Dennison / 42

His World / Larry Lefkowitz / 43

Ancient Wisdom / Jack Granath / 45

On Top of the World / Irene Buckler / 48

Nicotine / Mark Hudson / 50

Wise Folly / Lesley Middleton / 53

The Wise Owl / Jerry Vilhotti / 56

Best Bad Influence / Alex Reece Abbott / 57

Aristotle the Wise / Duff Allen / 59

Floaters / DL Shirey / 61

End Game / Louise Hofmeister / 64

The Big Mouth / Steven Carr / 67

The Independent Soul / Alex Robertson / 69

If I Had the Time / Sophie Van Llewyn / 72

Game Theory / Ruth Sabath Rosenthal / 76

Eating Rice Pudding with Simon /
Ruth Z. Deming / 78

Not-So-Fine Cotton / Mercedes Webb-Pullman / 80

On the Nature of the Choice of Our Nature /
Stephen V. Ramey / 84

Day Trip to Deaville / John Lambremont, Sr. / 87

My Mother, the Saint / Michael Marrotti / 90

Imperfect Company / John Grey / 94

Don't join the army, son / Martin Shaw / 96

Baseball Tonight / Wayne Scheer / 97

Stains / Jan Chronister / 100

Begot / Gwendolyn Joyce Mintz / 101

Authors / 103

About the Artist / 121

Commute

Claudia Bierschenk

A race of cyclists to the traffic lights.
Each worker wedged in to get an edge.

With steaming nostrils, balaclavas
We ready ourselves for the daily fight.

A red star lights up the front of my
black bicycle helmet.

(I might as well be in Siberia)

All these Berlin Winters have not
made me wiser in how to deal with the cold
that eats through two pairs of gloves.

Sometimes, it's colder on the inside.

Sometimes Electives Aren't

Paul Beckman

I enrolled in Wiser 101. My father insisted. It's embarrassing, I'm a junior in a freshman class, but he's not been pleased with my life decisions lately. The tattoo of The Last Supper with Harry Potter characters was his last straw. I don't know how many straws he started out with but I think it would've been fair to give me a two-straw warning similar to the two-minute warning in football.

He sprung this on me and I have to sit in this class. On day two of the class I got in fifteen minutes late and the teacher stopped his lecture and told the class why I was there in the first place and then asked me if upon reflection, I could have made a wiser decision and gotten to the class on time.

I told him that as far as I was concerned he did not make a wise decision in sharing my personal circumstances with the class and asked him if he can't make a wise decision regarding something as important as confidentiality, how can we believe him in modifying our habits so we make wise decisions?

He told me to think over what I said and try to come to a wise conclusion.

I thought it over and went to the dean and told him about the embarrassment of the teacher breaking confidentiality. He sat for a few minutes, chin in hand, hmming, and asked me to take off my shirt and show him the tattoo. I'm a big Harry Potter fan, he said.

Thrilled with the artwork as well as the subject matter he emailed my father and told him I no longer had to continue in Wiser since I've proven in a one-on-one to be wiser than the teacher.

Chickens

Len Kuntz

I am five or six and Mother is showing my brothers how to butcher chickens. They corral the squirming birds and Mother stretches each one's neck across a tree stump, raises her butcher knife and slashes down hard as black blood sprays the weeds. Once in a while she lets my brothers kick the headless carcasses in the ass, my brothers hooting while the dismembered chickens flop down the slope that leads to our trailer.

We have an early dinner where one of the butchered birds is served. The meat tastes like clay and I keep gagging. Mother says I will be whupped if I don't finish my plate, but I can't eat, so she gets out the strap to fulfill her promise.

Another day I watch Mother in the kitchen sifting through a box of wigs, trying them on over her real hair. There are blonde wigs and brunette wigs, some curly or straight, others blunt cuts. Once she's selected her favorite and clipped it into place, Mother sprays perfume in the air and walks through the mist looking like a mannequin.

The man who picks her up drives a car instead of a truck, and it has no dents. He wears a sweater with buttons and a black and white diamond pattern. He tries to peek inside our trailer, but Mother closes the door fast, her voice sounding different when she greets him, as if she's actually happy.

After she's gone, my brothers and I go outside because it's summer and the sun stays up late into the evening. Both Robbie and John grab their bb guns and start shooting at me, so I run. A couple of pellets nick me, one sticking in my neck like a dart. I dash through the lot behind our trailer, past abandoned refrigerators and rusted oil barrels. I bury myself under a compost pile, leaving just enough room to breathe. I hear my brothers yell my name, telling me come out of hiding, calling me a chicken, saying if I don't come out, I'm really going to get it. I let them go on until they give up, and even still, I wait beneath the rot.

*

I am forty-six and my mother's dead body sits inside the wooden box four feet away in front of me. Robbie and John are slumped beside me sobbing, while I can't muster a tear to save my life. I've flown two thousand miles to be here, but I could be anywhere.

Once the funeral services are over, the three of us stand in a parking lot.

Robbie blows his nose into a crumpled hanky and says, "Hell, let's grab some chow."

"Yeah," John says, "and Hot Shot here can pick up the tab."

I tell them I'm not hungry. I say I like to eat alone. I get in my car and drive.

Woefully Wiser

Jan Elman Stout

I last felt Sarah's nervous touch seconds before she tumbled ten feet below street level as the Metro-North subway train rumbled by. The heel of her stiletto had wedged in the sidewalk grate and she grabbed my arm for support. Tipping her foot one way and another, she slid free of the shoe right as the grate gave way. Arms windmilling, her eyes cut toward mine when the steaming maw snatched her.

I think of her and cry tears with no salt.

My mind sifts through data like a machine. The moving trains' roofs are two yards below the grate. A Metro-North train passes daily, at precisely 10:03. A live 13,000-volt transformer lays in wait, dead center.

Every day there are over nine million people in New York City. Someone falls through a grate every twenty months or so.

My Sarah.

I grabbed the shoe she abandoned at the scene, my only relic. I store it in a plain cardboard box tucked below the floorboards. She comes to mind and I polish it clean.

Christian Louboutin manufactured Sarah's nude stilettos. I know because hers match one of thousands of pairs in images I've scanned on the computer. Thousands of pairs but mine held her foot.

Sarah's eyes were the color of cornflowers. Although they might have been brown.

Her hair was red. Unmistakably. And wavy. Or straight.

The day she disappeared I wrote, "Sarah, come back, I love you," next to the grate. In white chalk, my heart exploding.

That night the rain stole my words; I wrote them again the next morning.

On clear days millions of feet trample and smudge my message. .000005 percent of those feet wear nude Christian Louboutin stilettos like my love. They negotiate the grate effortlessly, like dancers.

Pressing hard on the chalk, my fingers scrape the pavement as I meticulously retrace each letter. They fold tighter, concealing the leftover nub that dirties my clammy palm.

I'll repeat this ode to my love as long as I am able, for twenty months or so.

Dear Students

Martin Jon Porter

If I could teach poetry
all over again,

I'd steer clear
from the skill and drill
of ...

boring as bat shit
...

... that burr the soul

... of a mad man's mutterings

and mind-shushing
... .

But I would get you
to remember
just one personification:

What messages inside
the poet's stomach
are palpating?

Planet Fykaluxt

Allan J. Wills

He has an imaginary planet named Fykaluxt. "Not 'V', 'F'," he corrects. He waves vaguely to the eastern sky to indicate its position. "It's between the orbit of Pluto and Neptune," he says. He knows the order and nature of the planets in the solar system. We explore the planets on the NASA JPL web sites each evening after we go inside and he cleans his teeth.

This evening, I contemplate the sky with him. It will only take a small step of his imagination for him to consider that out there might be another planet where a father and son are looking up at the stars and weighing the same possibility of our existence. I'm patient enough to let him come to this discovery himself.

Carrying the rumination further, even scientists wiser than I could not refute the possibility, owing to the nature of our existence, that an infinite number of fathers and sons might be created moment to moment, unseen to themselves and yet so close.

Breaking my reverie, my son clasps my hand and says, "Carry me up, Dad."

Rogue Desire

Cynthia Leslie-Bole

She wanted the snap of eyes meeting across the club, the tension of seduction beginning, the rush of bodily contact on the dance floor, the shiver of man-breath on her neck, the delicious uncertainty of whether or not she would go home with a new specimen of maleness that night. She wanted to feel she was still in the game, wasn't too chubby or wrinkled, too older-but-wiser to flirt with the unknown.

That's what she wanted. But what Gladiola needed was different. She needed Joe, her ever-reliable husband, the man who shuffled to breakfast with his dry, cracked heels hanging off the back of his crumpled slippers, the one who married her in spite of three kids under the age of eight by three different lovers, the one she met in a laundromat while wearing sweats and no makeup—hardly the way she liked to present herself to men. But somehow this stripped-down beginning also wiped away the artifice Gladiola had relied on ever since she began her 'man career', as she called it, by seducing Jimmy Blackwell at the 9th grade prom. Joe caught her flat-footed, literally, without the six-inch heels that made her feel flush with power. And to her surprise, when he asked her to get coffee while their clothes swirled, she said yes, and she didn't pull away when his square, thick-fingered hand grabbed her manicured one as they walked back across the street to fetch their clean clothes. No suggestive throb of music, no alcohol to lubricate the interaction, no low lights to soften her face—just two unadorned people looking into each other. Gladiola felt naked with Joe in a whole new, uncomfortable way right from the beginning.

And they didn't even sleep together on their first night out, didn't even kiss. Gladiola didn't know what to make of it. She wasn't head-over-heels in love or even that attracted to Joe, but somehow his steady-Eddie presence soothed her in a way that some part of her sorely needed. So when he proposed without preamble in his earnest, simple way, she said yes. Her kids loved the guy, after all—who wouldn't when he baked them brownies and carved birds for them with his Swiss Army knife?

But what was she to do with the storms of desire that still raged in her? What was she to do about this dull, safe sameness that begged to be consumed by fire? What was she to do when she woke up drenched in the dream of an electric encounter, only to find the lump of Joe snoring peacefully beside her?

Gladiola knew that what she wanted was not what she needed, but what she wanted became all the more compelling as she tried to ignore the siren songs luring her toward shipwreck. The best she could do was snuggle up behind Joe, trying to curve her rogue desires as well as her body to this dear, kind man.

Wising Up

Rick Blum

It is often said that age brings wisdom, though usually by people who are more concerned with fending off osteoporosis than the number of Twitter followers they have. Myself, I can confidently proclaim that I am much wiser now than I was at 25, although that's not setting the bar very high. After all, at 25 I didn't give a second thought to getting up on a ladder to chop an ice dam off the roof, never pausing to think that when it let loose it would slide off the roof – taking down the ladder and me with it. Thanks to three-feet of fluffy snow, I was not hurt. But as a result, I am now wise enough to visualize everything that can possibly happen while up on a ladder, and decide to wait for spring.

The irony is that I thought I was much wiser back then, probably due to my youthful proclivity to employ

Rumsfeldian thinking, that is, I didn't know what I didn't know, so I assumed I knew everything. This approach gave me the confidence to attempt virtually any task no matter how uninformed I was of its subtleties or hazards. Today, I'm acutely aware of the many things I don't know, and consequently am often wise enough to avoid potential disasters.

For instance, I know I don't know how to wire a three-way dimmer switch solely because I once attempted this seemingly simple feat and had to be rescued by my father-in-law – the one with a Master's Degree in electrical engineering. It's not that I was reckless or inattentive; I was careful to turn off the power, and then mark each wire so I could reinstall them in the new switch exactly as in the non-functioning one. It's just that after doing so, the lights were no longer fully controllable from both switches, and I had not a clue why. I did have a few choice words to direct at the new switch, but not any idea as to how to fix it. As a result, I now keep the electrician's number on speed dial . . . right after the guy who specializes in clearing ice dams.

Truth is, the list of things I know I don't know is quite long. Among them are:

• When a high-flying stock has hit its peak
• The difference between ecru and taupe

- When a honeydew melon is ripe
- Whether a martini is better shaken or stirred
- When to shut up

And those are just the highlights of a list that seems to grow longer instead of shorter with each passing day. And for folks like me who have passed through youth and a good chunk of middle age, this is the ultimate source of wisdom: we know the most important what-we-don't-knows, and can regularly save ourselves from monumental screw-ups, as well as the embarrassment of sounding foolish expounding on things we simply don't know much about. Which leads me to wonder: Is it time to shut up?

18 Nots

Ron Campbell

I'm not on your agenda
We're not on the same page
We don't see eye to eye
I'm not acting my age
It's not for nothing that I say
The reason why is just because
I'm not the man I used to be
Maybe I never was.
It's not the first time this has happened
It's not the last by a long shot
Most the things I learned in life are not
      what I was taught
And all the things I'm thinking now are just
      not what I thought
'Cuz it's not where you are, it's where you are not.

It's not who you know it's the ones you forgot

It's not what you have it's what you've not got

I don't know who I am but I know who I'm not

I'm not knocking nothing if it's all that you've got.

The future gets the headlines while the past

      is left to rot

Now you're positive I'm negative

I get that a lot

But I'm not giving in and I'm not giving up

I'm not going quietly

I'm not some kind of chump

I guess I just won't take yes for an answer

The reason why is just because

I'm not the man I used to be.

Maybe I never was.

Crossing crossings

Piet Nieuwland

In star fabric night

Time collapses, a green canvas tent blustered

In summer hot-wet nor-easters

The past a ghost, palisaded

Deserted cottage, a church abandoned

From the balcony of a vanishing paradise

We become weightless

In the land of our viscous identity

The rivers memory, nano-fine steel

Enough of once was, used to be, then

Our lives are treasures, all passes

If we are to live here, wiser in this model world

A tomorrow is what we need

Where harakeke flowers bloom from our blood
From constitutional cliffs,
Cloud melting waterfalls billow and sheen
Between writing and speech, stars
        fall on contradictions
Of symbol, precise meaning and synaptic nuances
In plazas, patios, on riverbanks, remote mountain
Tops and cafés of now pragmatic-romantics
Karearea change to harakeke muka pendants
Taiaha sky hanging
Upon a zephyr's shoulder

Hallowed Halls

Todd McKie

From: Melody Barnstead, Dean of Student Affairs

To: All undergraduate and graduate students

Re: Professor Alan Tompkins

Dear MC Students,

Following his arrest, Professor Alan Tompkins has been placed on administrative leave. Students enrolled in his classes and needing assistance should contact Associate Professor Glenda Pinckney-Bennett at glenpb@manchester.edu

Professor Tompkins' records of mid-semester grades for both sections of LIT 207: Fiction, Farce, and Futility in the Medieval World, were destroyed in the fire. Indeed, it appears the grade sheets themselves were used to ignite the blaze. Gilchrist Hall remains closed for repairs until further notice.

The gender-inclusive restroom in the Wiggins Building has reopened after removal of extensive graffiti. Slogans such as "Make up your mind!" or "Show me yours!" have no place within an institution which values diversity and the dignity of all, without regard to genitalia.

In a related incident, Hancock Library reports several copies of Chaucer's *Canterbury Tales* have been defaced with drawings that Head Librarian Dorothea Frink calls "extremely rude." These volumes have been removed from circulation.

Members of the Manchester College community with information about events preceding the fire, unusual encounters with Professor Tompkins, photos or videos of the "streaking" incident and his "musical performance" in the dining hall are asked to contact

Cheryl Mahoney, Asst. District Attorney, at 617-839-4407 or cmahoney@middlesexda.gov

You may have heard rumors regarding the search of Professor Tompkins' home: reports of foul-smelling potions, a bloody hacksaw, dozens of pairs of size 11 ballet shoes, and numerous oil paintings of naked elderly men and women.

Police Chief Chester Ridley, admitting he is not an expert, said the paintings are, nonetheless, "in very poor taste." No hacksaw was found, but garden shears were recovered which Ridley believes were used in Professor Tompkins' self-mutilation.

The "potions" are OTC medications to combat sweaty palms, toenail fungus, and flatulence. These, along with a collection of Lionel Richie CDs and a hoard of Girl Scout Cookies are unrelated to any criminal activity. Chief Ridley declined to comment on the ballet shoes.

Following surgery for reattachment of his tongue, Professor Tompkns is undergoing court-ordered evaluation at a secure facility. He pleaded not guilty to charges of arson, destruction of property, indecent exposure, and disturbing the peace. An additional charge of animal cruelty was dismissed; the parrot has fully recovered and its owners have declined to press charges.

Alan Tompkins, despite his reputation as an "odd duck," served this College with distinction for many years. The Academic Disciplinary Council, co-chaired by myself and Nathan Guskowski, Dean of Faculty, will meet shortly to determine Professor Tompkins' continued role, if any, at MC.

Manchester College recognizes the emotional suffering caused by these unfortunate events. Our campus will continue to be a safe haven for reflection and healing. Together we will overcome this challenge and emerge wiser and stronger than ever. Our excellent faculty and staff will not be defined by the actions of one deeply troubled individual.

Sincerely,

Melody L. Barnstead, BA, MBA, DDS
Dean of Student Affairs
Manchester College

Miss Palmerston's Ring

Nod Ghosh

"She was sitting in a pool of her own piss singing *God Save the Queen*." Elizabeth had a way of sensationalising the mundane. *She* was Miss Palmerston our old biology teacher. Elizabeth had seen her outside Co-op muttering to herself, a line of drool on her chin.

"That's sad," I said, cupping the phone to my ear.

"Poor woman," Elizabeth added, though I could hear a smirk in her voice.

I hadn't intended any irony when I used the word *sad*, but I think Elizabeth heard it that way.

*

Miss Palmerston had spoken in circles. She taught less than you needed for exams, but more than you needed for life. She'd bang on the desk when we daydreamed. She shouted at us for manhandling the microscopes. We called her a rodent whilst dissecting rats, and stared at passing boys when she taught about fertilisation.

We didn't need her lecturing us. We were wiser than she was.

Elizabeth hated Palmy, especially after the woman ripped into her for confusing atrium with ventricle. She made her cry.

Elizabeth is a professor of anatomy now, and I wonder if Miss Palmerston was instrumental in making that happen.

*

Palmy wore a gold ring on the fourth finger of her right hand. It had a ruby in it.

Melanie Dawes once said, "That ring Palmy wears was an engagement ring." We'd sneaked into the sixth-form toilet for a smoke.

"Really?"

"Yeah. Her fiancé was killed in the war."

"Oh."

Our teachers had lost fathers or brothers in the war. Their stories lacked potency because we'd heard them so often.

I'd heard the engagement story before, but with different endings.

The prefects said Palmy's fella ran off with another woman.

The theatre group girls said he'd run off with a man.

We imagined it was the loss of her lover that aroused Miss Palmerston's rancour, but that didn't stop us bitching behind her back.

He's better off dead than being with her.

She's such a shrew, no wonder he left.

She looks like a man anyway with that moustache. He could have stayed with her if he was a homo.

*

When I was in sixth-form, my lover left me for my best friend.

It tore me apart.

In biology, I twisted Terry's ring on my finger. It wasn't gold, and it didn't have a ruby. I scribbled some words on my test paper.

Afterwards, Miss Palmerston asked if I was all right.

I said I was fine.

She said I could talk to her if I needed.

I walked away.

*

When Elizabeth called today, I didn't ask how Terry was. As she prattled on about her job, I wondered whether Miss Palmerston had found anyone to talk to when she needed them. I thought of her sitting on that cold pavement, her wits blown to shreds by some distant memory.

I thought about how we discredited her.

Yet she had been wise, probably wiser than any of us.

We just couldn't see it.

going dry at the poetry slam

Rob Walker

an entire day practicing the two pieces.
at the competition,
shy of half a minute in
scanning the audience
words dry up. a creek in summer.

there is nothing.
mind as blank as meditation.
a five second pause
uncomfortable for an audience
and me.

nothing works.
none of the word-associations,
the memory prompts,
hours of gabbled rehearsals.
i apologise and sit down.

and begin
to beat myself up
is the old anxiety returning?
am i getting alzheimers?
do i drink too much?

all the self-doubt of a lifetime
concentrated into one looped moment.
there's youtube evidence.
another loop for all the world
to see.

but on that same day
the bombs go off in Paris.
embarrassment and self-absorption pale.
the blessing-count
begins

Wisdom

Matt Dennison

"Nope, don't think
I'd much like having
th'bility to see the truth
behind everthang I done
in this life—might find
out I made a pot o' tea
onc't what had a roach
berld innit," he said
after drawing long
and slow on his
pipe.

His World

Larry Lefkowitz

At the funeral, I couldn't decide whether to bury with John the pin in the shape of a globe of the world suspended by a small chain which he had given me. In the end, I reasoned that it was too precious a reminder of him to do so. I kept it in my pocket, fingering it sadly during the ceremony.

As I turned from the grave following the burial, I passed a woman who still stood there, dabbing at her cheek with a handkerchief. But what caused me to almost faint on the spot was the pin she wore. A globe of the world suspended by a small chain – identical to that I felt in my pocket.

After I recovered from the shock, I approached her. "Excuse me, where did you get that pin?" I asked breathlessly.

"From John. A gift."

I reached into my pocket, my hand shaking, and took out my pin. I held it up. The globe swayed gently on its chain.

We both were rooted to the ground in shock.

I was the first to break the silence. "John told me he had this pin designed especially for me."

"He told me the same thing," she stammered.

"He told me when he gave it to me that I meant the world to him," I said.

"He used the exact same words when he gave me mine," she replied, almost in a whisper.

I slid my arm into hers. "We have a lot to talk about," I said.

She nodded.

We left the cemetery arm-in-arm.

Ancient Wisdom

Jack Granath

The party had moved to Fat Boy's unfinished basement, where five filthy sofas squatted on the cracked concrete beneath a welkin of irrational water pipes. Dozens of people lounged there or crowded around the wax-spattered ping-pong table or sulked in damp corners. A grown man was trying to get up a game of charades. A couple of comics walked around selling tickets to a plainly fictional puppet show, scheduled for two A.M. in a dangerous-looking crawl space. They were having a great time. Framed perfectly in one small, largely occluded, areaway window, a woman's legs leaned in a pool of yellow streetlight, black hose angling between a strip of miniskirt and a pair of shouting red pumps.

I discussed this fashion statement with an adolescent Carlyle, who explained it to me passionately, her unsurprising argument struggling against the pleasant stridency of some song du jour.

A willing laugh, a finger passed behind one ear. Crazy, I thought, and crushed out the conversation at once by betting, with an air of malicious flirtation, that I was twice her age. I lost, but not by much. Not by enough. Her winnings amounted to a small act of aiding and abetting in the delinquency of a minor. She took her beer and went off.

I was just there for the drugs.

But that laugh went to work, as I knew it would. That laugh and that tentative gesture. I sat there enjoying it, actually basking in the warmth still radiating from this small, friendly moment I had hurried on its way. Then I realized: it was something Hannah used to do when she was nervous, that simultaneous tuck and laugh with maybe a sideways look. And I used to make her nervous. Imagine.

Finally, Fat Boy showed up at his own house and I scored. The evening proceeded, if non-sequentially, and I holed up to watch it unfold. The puppet show petered out. Someone threw up in his obliging girlfriend's lap. The legs were still framed in that miserable little window, and I realized, with an everyday sense of loss, that someone had painted them there.

Eventually, the young came at me again, Alex, from the diner, and his pack of aspiring rock star friends. Good kids, for the most part, who saw themselves as discoverers: new music, new poetry, new frontiers. The girl was with them, drinking someone else's beer. She didn't acknowledge me, except to smirk a little when Alex offered his usual salutation, "Hey old man, hit us with some of that ancient wisdom."

I usually answered with whatever was knocking around in my head, a fragment of nonsense or an old rhyme. This time though, I took the matter more seriously. I gave it a vicious five seconds of thought.

"Time heals all wounds," I said at last, then laughed like a lunatic in an old movie, like a mad scientist on the brink of conquest or destruction, laughed until they were all pretty scared.

On Top of the World

Irene Buckler

The view from the summit is breathtaking. The city far below is a Lilliputian jewel against a majestic coastline that meanders into the distance.

"Worth the climb?" he asks.

Out of puff from the last and steepest part of their ascent, she simply nods.

They stand together on the lofty rocky outcrop, defying the biting wind that nips at their faces and fingers, his arms encircling her protectively from behind, she leaning back into the secure warmth of his embrace.

As their wedding anniversary approached, she had been both surprised and delighted when he had suggested the climb – just the two of them, a chance to get away from everyone else and reconnect. Although not a climber, she recognised that having time alone was just what they needed to revitalise their struggling marriage and now, at this very moment, on top of the world, they are as one again.

"I love you," she murmurs.

His arms clamp tightly around her as he lifts her off her feet and nobody hears her scream as she plummets to her death.

He is comforted by their friends and family after the tragic loss of his wealthy young wife, but they are none the wiser. They think they understand when, heartbroken, he announces his intention to relocate to Hawaii. But they know nothing.

Nicotine

Mark Hudson

I was in a writers group I facilitated a couple of years back. The writing prompt came up, "What is one thing in life you hope you never do again?"

This woman and I unanimously said, "I hope I never smoke cigarettes as long as I live."

We talked about it, and how we quit, and a young person in the group, who seemed to have his
   act together,
who seemed to be writing for blogs, television shows, and (gasp! getting paid! talk about really humbling) said, "You mean, you used to smoke cigarettes, and you talk about it as if it's just some casual, everyday thing?"

When I was growing up in the 1970's in America,
everybody smoked. It was advertised everywhere.

Farther back in the fifties, tobacco was really popular.
My father confessed that in third grade him and
        his friends
would steal their parent's cigarettes, and go into an
abandoned house and smoke!

    Like father, like son, I started my addiction
in third grade, too. In those days they had
        cigarette machines,
so they were easy to sneak and race out of the store, and
run to the park and smoke them.

    I have not had a cigarette since the year 2000. But
I was a chimney, smoking two and a half packs a day.

As far as being wiser, I thought I was going to write
a story about my history of wearing glasses. But I used to
be so embarrassed about all the dumb things I did in high
school, but that was thirty years ago, and people used to
say, "Whatever happened to Hudson?" But I'm sure
nobody from my graduating class of high school is
thinking of me, and I'm certainly not thinking of them!

I quit smoking through a local stop smoking clinic that no longer exists. I think about how bad I smell right now writing at this computer, (I didn't take a shower today, and it's the American holiday of Valentine's day, the day of romance and flowers, and I have no significant other, so why take a shower? Besides, when I used to have girlfriends, I'd work hard, or whatever, then I'd go to see them, and they'd say, "You stink!" and they didn't realize they did too, I'd been working, and they'd been sitting around smoking, and they stunk, too, probably slept with a side lover too, while I was working, so celibacy is also a new-found form of wisdom!) And lastly, sorry kiddies, vaping is not a safe alternative for smoking. Stressed out? Put on some headphones, bang your head, and let it go ... you'll be all the wiser.

Wise Folly

Lesley Middleton

First impressions weren't good for either of us. At the wedding reception, we were sparring almost continuously. He was opinionated, over-confident and clearly thought himself irresistible to women. I was argumentative and feeling jaded and cynical having recently ended a volatile relationship. He laughed at my sage response to something one of our fellow guests said, mockingly telling her to "wise up and learn from her elders." I realised then that I was kidding myself if I thought I could pass as part of their generation.

Later, as I said goodbye to the bride and groom, I heard a voice say, "How are you getting home?" I turned round, thinking the question had been directed to me. It hadn't. I watched as Gerry, the tall, attractive, self-assured American who had dominated the conversation at our table walked up to a pretty blonde who had been sitting with us.

"I'm going into the centre of town if that's any good to you?"

The blonde declined. She had her own car.

I heard myself saying, "I'd be glad of a lift into town, if you're offering." I smiled as engagingly as I could.

"Of course. My pleasure."

Gerry's car was a smart, red open-top Mazda sports job. Showy and ostentatious, I thought. Just like him.

After the first few miles I started to relax as we shared anecdotes about the bride and groom. It wasn't long before we were both helpless with laughter.

"I don't think we got off to a very good start at the reception," he said during a lull in the conversation. "Perhaps we should start again? I'm Gerry Lee."

"I'm Clare Jackson."

We shook hands and I felt a strange warmth surge through me. Gerry's eyes gazed into mine for far too long and the car momentarily veered off the road.

"Oops, better try and concentrate!" Gerry mimed the actions of an earnest, over-anxious driver, hunching over the steering wheel and gripping it with both hands, tongue protruding as though in deep concentration.

We didn't stop laughing until we reached the outskirts of the city. The warmth within me had turned into a feeling of excited fluttering.

"Shall we meet up again sometime?" Gerry asked.

My innate common sense suddenly kicked in. I felt something close down within me. What a fool I'd been. This would go nowhere, as had all my previous relationships. In fact it would be doomed from the start; I must be nearly twenty years older than him.

"I could do with a bathroom break," Gerry said, as he parked on the street where I live.

We walked to my flat in silence. I showed him the bathroom and went into the kitchen to put the kettle on.

I felt a movement behind me and turned. He took me in his arms. His kiss left me dizzy.

No strings, no expectations, I told myself firmly. Nothing serious.

But I wasn't listening. What harm could there be? I'm wiser now – aren't I?

The Wise Owl

Jerry Vilhotti

After a half hour, Johnny returned to Linda Ann drenched with sweat; suggesting it wasn't going to be as easy as he thought; mentioning the three places that had seen his desperation and had jacked up their prices a third and then when he said his wife was with him the sleeping price went up to double — way over the thirty-five dollars he had budgeted for each night's sleep in San Miguel Allende. He began to think Mexico was paying "his" people back for all the abuse it had done on them; beginning with guys like Davie Crooket, Bowie Knife, Sammy the Houston and sundry others too many to mention who bit off a chunk of Mexico for lots of money. He knew now he was the wiser.

Best Bad Influence

Alex Reece Abbott

Was there a full moon, or is she making that up? Thirty-odd years ago, they queued in the sweet, summer dusking, led astray again.

Drinking in the warm air, greasy with deep-fried doughnuts and candy-floss sticky. Technicolor lights were pulsing to the bass rock thrum, silhouetting the sentinel palms along The Esplanade.

Ever ready to sneak away from reality, every outing with Annie fizzed with adventure. She, more amusing than all the amusements; so tall, so blonde, hooded eyelids shaded the latest turquoise, like that girl from Abba. Knowing it all. Lee, ten years younger, a dark, unmade teenager. The kid sister, happy to observe and blend into the crowd: knowing it was impossible alongside Annie. Adrenaline-hooked, Annie seized the Rebel cap early, wore it threadbare. Nine years later, when Lee arrived, their parents assigned her ill-fitting Sensible.

That night, they rode the soaring Big Dipper, again and again, thinking they'd do it forever. Swooping, plummeting, on the verge of losing control. For all their differences, no barrier between them. That Luna Park night, gripping the cool, chrome safety bar, sliding, arms and legs entangled, one squealing, crushing mass.

The oldest now, Lee wonders why she didn't bring her camera that night.

The memory is breaking down like a Polaroid snap. Lee smiles, head bowed by all that's unspoken. Too late to tell Annie how even at her wildest and most rebellious, she made her laugh.

Such an instinct, to know how to live, best bad influence. Lee can still hear her laughter floating through that warm, sweet night.

Aristotle the Wise

Duff Allen

Some people, when the name "Aristotle" is spoken equate that immediately with the meaning of the word philosopher. And that word itself – philosopher – is heard by many as meaning to mean to engage in a sort of ongoing idleness, or a sort of meaningless, or at best neutral banter that really has no serious impact or effect on anything. And when the idea of philosophizing between two people in conversation eventually comes up, it means, generally, that we have been going on too long about something, like thinking about which of five movies on the marquee we should go to, so let's just stop talking about it, let's wrap it up, and pick one.

Even fewer understand that almost every single movie that is a Hollywood box office success is built on the observant details defined and made up originally by Aristotle himself, primarily in his handful of chapters known as his Poetics. Far fewer know that what he says about friendship, that a friend is a selfsame other, is one of the shining diamonds of the world. In other words, what I am saying is one of the most valuable utterances made by a man the world has ever known has lost its worth.

Floaters

DL Shirey

I noticed floaters whenever the room was lit; particles danced in the periphery, my vision framed by ghostly specks.

Long before I knew them better, an ophthalmologist explained. She palmed a plastic replica the size of a grapefruit, popped apart each nested section of the eyeball and placed them on a stainless steel tray. As a fleet of half-orbs rocked upon flat metal, the doctor held one up.

"Between the lens and retina is a viscous layer," she said, turning the opaque bowl before me.

My floaters followed the motion of her hand, lurching gelatinously whenever my eyes moved.

"As we age, small clots form, becoming thicker. When they congeal, light causes shadows to fall across the retina. That's all they are. Shadows. Nothing to worry about."

That was before I understood floaters, the way they clustered, their purposeful formations. Individually they are elongated, amoeba-like, sometimes segmented like worms. But it's their ability to pair, or group, and retain specific shapes that captured my attention.

Early in my studies, floaters loitered at the edge of my visual field, occasionally sending troops across the center as if relaying messages to the other side. The more I looked for them, the more there were, like ants at a picnic.

My many months of diagramming movement and sketching shapes were recorded in a journal, a thousand pages of scrupulous notes and detailed drawings. Their patterns were eventually revealed to be hieroglyphs and, as if the floaters knew how much wiser I had become, increased in volume and choreography. Now, my every waking moment was filled with scrawling in my journal.

To keep up with all these tantalizing clues, I reduced the size of illustrations and kept my tiny annotations brief. I began using a magnifying glass to ensure that my citations, small as they were, were always accurate.

The variations were staggeringly complex, until one day the floaters themselves came to my aid. It was as if they realized so many shapes had been deployed and wanted to help me focus on those at the very center of my vision. My companions darkened the frame and illuminated the masterpiece, and I was finally able to decipher a message. The Rosetta Stone moment.

My joy brought tears as the first full translation crawled across my eyes. The floaters were talking to me!

In my excitement to record the moment, my hands groped for the pen and magnifying glass. I found and grabbed them, but could not locate my journal. The floaters seemed just as anxious to communicate as they crowded my periphery, blacking out the room.

As I stared straight ahead only a pinprick of brightness was left to me, but still enough to see: *We're here. Don't worry*, the floaters declared, *the book is to your left.*

End Game

Louise Hofmeister

I woke relieved to find
you gone again.
A nurse peered down;
a friend held my hand.
I dumbly oriented.

Still tethered, muzzled
by those tubes, I knew
nothing I could do would
quench my thirst
or halt unceasing noise.

I closed my eyes returning
to our recent rendezvous.
You dropped a curtain as you left,
but still I felt you close.

I will be celebrated soon with
tales of extra hours needed,
giant tumors intertwined,
or vessel walls ballooning.

Was it brave of me to steer
beyond the usual frontiers
where one can talk to angels,
(or was that halogen humming
"You are loved?")

Rebuffed again, you must be sore.
Oh, I will cheat you when I'm able,
my tireless champions duel
with more than simple scalpels.

But since we've played at this so long
perhaps i'll change direction—
the wiser goal's not your defeat
but mastering resurrection.

The Big Mouth

Steven Carr

Danny didn't know how to keep his big mouth shut.

I was sitting at the bar and Danny was sitting on his favorite stool next to me. He was pushing around the maraschino cherry in his drink with the thinly-sliced half an orange garnish when a guy I'd never seen before sat down on the stool on the other side of Danny. The guy was large; very tall and extremely bulky with the head the size of a small watermelon. Watching Danny in the mirror behind the bar I knew immediately there was going to be trouble. Danny had a gambler's tell. He ran his hand through his thick red hair just before saying something rude.

"Your mother must have loved giving birth to you," Danny said to the guy.

The guy looked down at Danny and said, "You talking to me?"

Danny picked up the cherry with his fingertips and popped it in his mouth and bit down on it. "Yeah, I am," Danny said looking up at the guy. "Giving birth to you couldn't have been easy."

"What business is it of yours if my birth was easy or not?" the guy said.

Danny gulped his drink. "None," he said, "except you'd be a great advertisement for birth control."

If Danny couldn't see it coming, I could. The guy stood up and towering over Danny he drew back his massive fist and smashed it forward right into Danny's grinning mouth. He landed on the floor with a thud. Two of his front teeth slid across the tiles.

A few weeks later I was in the bar sitting on the stool. Danny sat down next to me. He ordered a whiskey sour and while sipping it looked at the mirror and grinned, revealing the gap where his two teeth had been.

A short time later a guy with an enormous nose sat down next to Danny. Danny looked at the guy and ran his hand through his hair, and I could tell that he was about to say something, but he put the cherry in his mouth and said nothing.

The Independent Soul

Alex Robertson

The one who explores
An inquisitive being
    Independent of society
A self-declared hermit
Operating within a culture set
That few fully understand
Using books and the internet vigilantly
To uncover the secrets of life
Asking questions of family
    and acquaintances on occasion
Using discretion

(Knowing that Led Zeppelin tune
    where there are two meanings)
To become sage
    against those wielding knowledge
For their own benefit
Ruses and rubicons to taunt and deceive
Putting them in the box seat
    (in this life)
Or on the stage of humanity's performance
To be forever remembered

A fear of the other
Not necessarily playing with the full deck
Arcane thoughts when sorting them
But the connected play cards in opposition
Holding their hand close
Betting trumps to suit their purposes
Seeing how many tricks they can perform
Before the game is over
Waving a wand of superiority over the table
To put the cup before them
Life can overflow with positive interaction
Rather than dealing in spells of concentration
Of benefit to all and sundry
Rather than a penchant for a single outcome

"No swords seen before me"
As the loner sits high on the hill
More a track for The Cardigans than The Beatles
Intelligence a qualitative matter
Worldly or esoteric
Lived experience a hip-gnosis
Getting wiser by the day
    by seclusion or in public arenas
One soul versus the world

If I Had the Time

Sophie Van Llewyn

The winter sun is as cold as the blade of a knife. I wish I had time to put a jacket on before stepping out onto the balcony, but I might miss a single word between her, my next door neighbour, and the hippie who runs the bakery. She is swinging her pram seductively, back and forth, in the rhythm of her hips, while he is pushing a chai latte over the counter. On the house, presumably. I found out that he's giving her stuff for free when I happened to stand in line behind her. I decided to leave nothing more to chance — so I bought the binoculars and learned how to read lips.

*

Cup in one hand and pushing the pram with the other, she is passing Mr. Johnson, who's cleaning the snow off the driveway. She's all smiles and a flapping of blonde curly hair. Mr. Johnson is melting worse than the snow. I could have looked like that too, after giving birth, if I had a rich husband like hers, to pay for a private trainer and weekly sessions at the hairdresser's.

At noon, I'm cooking, but I keep running onto the balcony. Bert's shoes, cramming the hallway, slow me down. I wish he had taken them with him when he left. I ditch the half-cooked pasta sauce in a bag and fry some eggs. After I eat, I do a routine check and I want to slap myself for my negligence. At my age, I should be wiser. She's now gone — I catch the rustle of her beige coat in the distance. I wait. Soon, she's returning. She has a new hat. Gucci. I could have bought posh hats when I was young, too, if I didn't have to raise two children.

*

I step back inside as my doorbell rings. I try to catch my rushing breath and make myself invisible. She insists.

"Mrs. McLeroe? Open up, I know you're home! I've seen you on the balcony!"

In person, she's even taller. I could have been so, too, if my parents had given me vitamins.

"Could I please have some sugar?" she says. "I want to bake a pie."

I used to bake pies, too, for my Bert, but now I can't find the time.

I chase away a few flies as I open the cupboard. There is a tower of dishes where my kitchen sink used to be. I rinse one of the mugs in the bathroom.

"You know what, Mrs. McLeroe? I've changed my mind. I'll just buy something from the bakery," she says, breathing oddly through her mouth.

"I bet you will," I say, as I close the front door.

*

I look at the dozen garbage bags, surrounding the overflowing bin, at the layer of breadcrumbs on the floor, at the traces of dirt and something sticky in the hallway. I could clean up, too, and have a house as shiny as hers. But who would watch her, then?

Game Theory

Ruth Sabath Rosenthal

Nanny approached me and I thought it was
about the baby — whether to bathe him now
or later. Instead, she told me she had to leave.

Okay, what time will you be back? In contrast to
her usual sheepish manner, she practically screamed
You don't understand. I need to go for good.

Please don't try to change my mind. I was shocked.
Had I somehow offended her? She assured me
it wasn't anything I'd done or said, but wouldn't say

why she was leaving. That made no sense, until
decades later when I, too, fled, having finally fathomed
her leaving was likely my husband's doing. That wolf,

no doubt, had fancied the dear girl fair game. Not a stretch
of imagination considering he'd also once fancied me
over the woman he'd been married to at the time.

Eating Rice Pudding with Simon

Ruth Z. Deming

I pick my prettiest bowl
a gift from Helene before
she went to the old ladies'
home and spoon in the
Rice Pudding from
Altamonte's Market.

The aroma of cinnamon
and vanilla and perhaps
of heavy cream tantalizes
me, as it does Simon.

We sit at the kitchen table
exchanging loving looks and
"Ain't this delicious!" he
liked speaking in poor grammar
with his genius IQ

A curmudgeon is what he was,
wiser and sillier than any man
I've ever met, coming downstairs
late at night to watch television
and leave cheese and cracker
crumbs for me to vacuum
the next morning

We'd eat Rice Pudding at the
Eagle Diner, Bonnet Lane,
and way over at Lancer's on
Street Road

Who says you can't eat Rice
Pudding with a dead man? He
comes around when he feels
like it and I welcome him
with a kiss.

Not-So-Fine Cotton

Mercedes Webb-Pullman

I'm pencilling at Randwick, the Rails, working
on Brisbane races, Eagle Farm meeting that day.
There's a sort of low buzz going around the track,
'Someone's got a fix in' but that's not unusual,
there's always some cheating going on, I'm not
curious about who or what or where, just keep
my head down and listen.

Punters want to back some knackery-bait in a race
at Eagle Farm. The early market shows fifty to one,
but The Boss doesn't want a cent of it. Even I know
something's off when every punter and his brother
wants to back the same long-priced roughie. It's got

no form, no wins, no chance of winning. Some owner
with more money than sense keeps sending it around
the tracks, and as long as it's registered, all fees paid,
it can run. Even though trainers hate wasting time,
it's owners with dreams who pay their bills.

Opening market has Fine Cotton at thirty-three to one.
Most bookies put up seven to two. Punters hurl abuse
as they sprint up and down the line, trying to get set
before every bookie has turned the price in. Next call
it's eight to one; bookies working the race go odds on,
and stay there when the call before they jump has it at
seven to two. The favourite's price has blown all the way
out to the Black Stump.

Of course the horse sprints out of the field after the jump
and chases down the favourite. He hardly crosses the line
when a roar goes up, on every race track in the country so
I'm told, and as far away as betting shops in Darwin, and
Fiji, of Ring-In! Ring-In! about the worst-kept secret
in the racing world ever. The punters abuse The Boss
as if he's part of it. He laughs, but his eyes turn very
black.

Turns out some in his family are warned off racetracks
all over the country for this, and lose their licences too.

The mysterious 'they' plan for a long time to win this race
with a ring-in for Fine Cotton; they buy a horse, almost
identical colour and markings, and set everything up.
Before the race their ring-in is injured, no way can it win.
The word's already out, there's some large investments
made by some hard people who will be very angry. 'They'
panic a bit, send for a new horse, buy Bold Personality,
not cheap but he can definitely win the race. Wrong
colour? A few bottles of Lady Clairol
turns bay into brown, though bleach
on his hind legs to make white patches
doesn't work. By now, hours before starting time,
they're convinced they have no choice, and open
that can of white paint.

Seems odd to me, very unsophisticated for this family.
Who paints a horse? It goes to weigh-in dripping paint.
Even Eagle Farm stewards have to take some action.
They tell bookies not to pay out on the race. There's
a riot brewing. Everyone knows the real story, and
they're all different.

The contrast in time sticks in my mind. Ninety seconds
of race time, then decades of court cases, wasted lives,
ruined careers, marriages, other relationships as well.
I can't decide if it's just cheeky, Aussie larrikin style,
or if it's really cheating. Whether Father O'Dwyer,
for example, would call it a sin.

On the Nature of the Choice of Our Nature

Stephen V. Ramey

We were concupiscent that day. It was in us, the fire, desire, murder for hire. Up and down the stairs we went, pairs of us creased with that sordid lust that drives boys. We wanted girls, dogs with bad teeth, justice for the unjust among us. We wanted greed.

Doors were locked. Fathers walled up their daughters. We had no keys, no chisels, only eyes to guide us, legs to carry us, penises hanging commando-style. Wilted as they were, the soil remained intact, that rich loam of do-not-want-to-die-alone packed with seeds ready to spring. To boil.

Jason crumpled first. Onto the landing he knelt, hands wrapping Eric's ankles, pulling him down too. Grunts, a scream, the sound of pants sliding.

Skin flashes in half-light and I am here beyond the experience. I want to pound Jason senseless, pound and pound and pound. Henry holds me back. I feel the tension in his grip.

"They made their choice," he says as he tugs me down step by step. I let myself be led to the next landing. I feel frustrated, but also grateful.

"It wasn't Henry's choice," I manage.

"Doctor Carson says it's a choice."

"To be brought down like a zebra? To be raped by his once-best friend?" I cover my ears briefly against the animal sounds. *StopitStop! Don'tbesuchafaggot.*

"He didn't have to walk with Jason," Henry says. He glances down. I shudder and yank my hand from his. The grunting takes on a rhythmic cadence. I want to look, which makes me want to vomit.

"Doctor Carson is a great neurosurgeon."

"Did he choose to be black? Did he choose to be smart?"

"Of course," Henry says with a firm nod. "Everything is a choice. That's why Jesus died."

"Jesus didn't die." A flush rises through me, a flooding warmth like the Nile overflowing its bank.

"'Course he did," Henry says. "And He came back to life. It was a miracle *and* a choice."

An image comes to me of a cave mouth, a stone pushed aside, a vaginal canal, a woman with legs spread wide. Was that a choice? I suppose it was. A string of connected pearls.

And I know in this instant that time is solid. There are no choices, only misunderstood inevitabilities. The fire in me will burn me down because it has, because it will have, because it must.

The struggle stops. For a few heartbeats silence hangs around us. Then, sounds of dressing, a metallic zip, and Jason clomps downstairs, followed by Eric, looking sheepish.

Are you all right? I want to ask. *Do you want me to kill him?*

Eric shrugs as if reading my mind. "I didn't know." And they walk past us, hand-in-hand, down the next flight into the dark recesses of a mind we can never comprehend.

"Speaking of choice." Henry loosens his belt. I think I thought I had known all along what would happen next.

Day Trip to Deaville

John Lambremont, Sr.

If you ever have to cross
the state line to go to Deaville,
there are a few things
you should know before you go.

The town is both the creation
and the victim of the plastics plant
and boosted and betrayed it;
the decayed art-deco architecture
of the old townhouses and downtown
reflect its past swells in population,

but few live there anymore;
the plant was shut down by the EPA,
and all but the poor and afflicted
have long since moved away.

Dr. DeMerritt is a kindly old soul,
and he fits his poisoned patients,
limp limbs ground down to stumps,
with prostheses fashioned
from the same synthetic,
blast-heated to inert form,
that poured for years through leaky valves
and broken pipes, and leached
into the groundwater below;
but the clinic shares a building
with the jail; be careful
what door you enter
and let close behind you;
you might have a hard time
talking your way out.

When it is time to leave,
turn right and right and right again,
as that is the only way out of town;
a left turn anywhere will lead
to a series of Do Not Enters
and Dead Ends, and you will
end up right back where
you started from again;

and whatever you do,
never enter the tunnel;
it is inhabited by subterraneans
that for varying sham reasons
never got even a small share
of the class action settlement;
they are unruly beyond resentment,
and will gladly stop your car
and molest you, or worse.

My Mother, the Saint

Michael Marrotti

The woman
has been married
three times
and divorced twice
yet takes no
responsibility
for her actions

My mother the saint
always portrays
herself as the victim

She gave birth
to a daughter
and a son
through this
second marriage
yet hasn't talked
to either in years
she's still portraying
herself as the victim

It must be an act
of convenience
an extra perk
that goes along
with the excessive
drinking

Blacking out
remembering
nothing
her own
shaky finger
pointing
in the opposite
direction

I'm a demon spawn
to her neighbors
and coworkers
pity on tap
she's infallible
the woman
has a way with
fiction

I'm telling you
my mother
excels at her craft
she's had her
entire life to practice
even my own kids
tell me I have to be
nice to grandma

I've given up
on diplomacy
long ago
once I realized
there's no cure
for the redundant

I'm a terrible
son of a bitch
member of the
guilty party
or better yet
a son of a drunk
who learned
from the best
how not to keep
his mouth shut

Imperfect Company

John Grey

Gale, not you,
I'm the one who's not here.
At first,
my absence
was a revelation,
stealing alone into myself,
and my eyes, my mouth,
no wiser.
But you wish to be seen and heard.
You stay close to my body,
awaiting my return.
But I'm elusive.
Even when I think of you,

we're not together.
You're seventeen and lovely.
You're twenty-five and staring over
the railing of a ship.
And where am I?
In this curse of a disappearing act.
Imagine and the world absolves me
of all reason.
Contemplate all but the here and now
and I wash up like a shell
on yesterday's shore,
shine a selfish light on tomorrow.
You hold me,
a wise choice
if I weren't already in my grip.

Don't join the army, son

Martin Shaw

See, a bayonet has grooves, so it is easy to pull back: no suction you see. They stab at high speed, twisting like a porn queen for a finale. Dead from the stomach down, you will scream 'blue murder'. And he will shout back as he lifts with each thrust, blessed are those taken by brutality, this is your destiny.

Your eyes will close, like the powdery wings of a moth, harvested for golden pigment.

Baseball Tonight

Wayne Scheer

Fats Lamar, the Lima Titans' aging manager, cursed to himself as he filled out the lineup card for the night game. They had just played an afternoon game and lost 4-3 in the eleventh inning. He kept scratching out names with his stub of a pencil when Gordon Leftmiller, his star center fielder, hobbled by.

"How you feeling, Gordy? You need a rest?"

"I'm okay, Fats. I can play tonight."

"You look like shit."

"I don't get paid for my looks."

"Good thing."

Leftmiller flashed his baby-faced smile. Lamar growled.

"I'm okay, really."

"That's not what doc thinks. He says you're pretty banged up."

"Guess I am. But ain't nothin' broke."

"'Cept maybe your head. Doc says he drained enough fluid from your right knee to fill a bathtub."

"Yeah. That made it good as new. Gave me a shot. I feel like a kid."

"You are a damn kid. Whata you? Nineteen?"

"Be twenty this winter."

"Sheeeiiit. I got jockstraps older'n you. Smell better, too."

"Yeah, but your jock ain't gonna cover center."

"What about your wrist? Lemme see."

Leftmiller dangled his right wrist in Lamar's face.

"Don't be a wise ass." The manager grabbed his player's left hand.

The kid grimaced.

"Still swollen. And it's the color of tobacco spit. Can you even grip a damn bat?"

"Sure. Besides, bunting's my game. You know that."

"But then you gotta run on that bum knee."

"Look, Fats. Some big league scouts may be watching us tonight. They don't care I went 3 for 5 with two steals today. All they gonna see is what I do tonight."

"Shit. You think scouts are out there watching us when they could be at their hotel eating expense account steak and screwing expense account whores?"

"Yeah, I do. That's why I play like nothin' else in the world matters."

The manager took a deep breath, puffed his cheeks and exhaled slowly. "Okay. You're leading off and playing center. But if your damn knee pops out, don't send your Momma after me."

"Thanks. Hey, Fats. Let me ask you since you're so wise, why you still managing after all these years?"

Fats looked up at his center fielder. "'Cause nothin' else matters."

Stains

Jan Chronister

Riding home from a shopping trip,
wearing her new Victoria's Secret blouse,
the one she saved for, had plans for,
my daughter drips chocolate ice cream down her front.

I console her with cold water and promises of bleach.
Back home I scrub and curse at God.

Later, married, wiser,
she calls with news of cystic fibrosis,
dead pets and tumors.

We talk out the spots the best we can,
sanitizing stains with our words.

Begot

Gwendolyn Joyce Mintz

Ben Whatley believed he'd never be considered a rich man with just two slaves to his name. He had an idea but when he told Travis the plan, he was met with a look of contempt and then an adamant shake of his male servant's head.

"You will," Whatley told him, "or I'll shoot her right before your eyes."

Travis did what he thought his heart could bear. Was it the wiser choice? His fingers lingered over the tie to her gown until he heard a gun cock.

Travis wept that first time and those following.

Anna, the other slave, was confused, frightened by it all. Why those times Mr. Whatley was at the door.

She'd cry herself, later, begging Travis to look at her, to talk to her, though the silence between them only grew as her belly did.

By the time the child was born, dead, there were no tears left. Anna simply buried the boy next to their daddy, under the tree where Travis had finally hanged his grief.

Authors

Alex Reece Abbott

writes across genres, forms and hemispheres. Her literary novel, *The Helpmeet*, was a 2016 *Greenbean Irish Novel Fair* winner. Her story *By-stander* features in the *Word Factory's Citizen* season. A finalist in the *2017 Bath Novella-in-Flash Award*, her stories have won the *Arvon*, *Crediton* and *Northern Crime* prizes. Widely published and anthologised, her short fiction often shortlists, including for the *Bridport, Elbow Room*, *Lorian Hemingway* and *Sunday Business Post/Penguin Short Story* prizes.

Duff Allen

is a writer who lives in upstate New York. He has an MFA from Bard College where he teaches writing in The Clemente Course for the Humanities. His work appears in *Prima Materia, Burningword Literary Journal, Eunoia Review*, and many other publications.

Paul Beckman

has been widely published, in the following magazines among others: *Connecticut Review*, *Raleigh Review*, *Litro*, *Playboy*, *Pank*, *Blue Fifth Review*, *Flash Frontier*, *Matter Press*, *Metazen*, *Thrice Fiction* and *Literary Orphans*. His work has been in a number of anthologies and a dozen countries. Paul was one of the winners in the 2016 Best of the Small Fictions. He's the author of two story collections, *Peek* and *Come! Meet My Family and other stories*, a novella, *Lovers and Other Mean People* and a chapbook of flash and micro stories, *Maybe I Ought to Sit in a Dark Room for a While*. He blogs at www.pincusb.com.

Claudia Bierschenk

has been published by *Juice Press*, *Full of Crow*, *A little poetry*, *Durable Goods*, *SAND Journal*, and anthologies by *Pure Slush*. Her first chapbook *Perestroika Silence* was published by erbacce Press, Liverpool in 2010. Her second chapbook *Luther* was published by PigEar Press, UK. Her work also features in poetry anthologies by Forward Press (UK) and the renowned Tangerine Press (UK). Claudia lives in Berlin with her son.

Rick Blum

has been chronicling life's vagaries for more than 25 years as a nightclub owner, high-tech manager, market research mogul, and old geezer. His poems and essays have appeared in *Humor Times*, *Boston Literary Magazine*, and *The Satirist*, among others. Currently, he is holed up in his office trying to pen the perfect bio, which he plans to share as soon as he stops laughing at the sheer futility of this effort.

Irene Buckler

taught in Australian primary schools for three decades, during which time she wrote many educational programs, stories for children and poetry, which have appeared in publications for children in the United Kingdom and in Australia. A flash fiction finalist in 2016's Hysteria (UK) and Field of Words Writing Competitions (South Australia), Irene's flash fiction stories may be found in various magazines and anthologies, in print and online.

Ron Campbell

is an actor and poet based in San Francisco, California where he acts in theatre and films when not touring the world with Cirque du Soleil. He is the author of the titles of two unwritten collections of poetry *The Detourist* and *In Corrigible* and his work has appeared in *Versus Pure Slush Vol. 4, Psychic Meatloaf, Flutter Poetry Journal* and *Mipoesia*. For more about Ron and his work, visit https://soarfeat.wordpress.com and www.soarfeat.org.

Steven Carr

began his writing career as a military journalist and has had over seventy short stories published internationally in print and online magazines, literary journals and anthologies. His plays have been produced in several American states. He was a 2017 Pushcart Prize nominee. He lives in Richmond, Virginia and writes full time. Find him on Facebook at https://www.facebook.com/profile.php?id=10001296 6314127 and Twitter @carrsteven960.

Jan Chronister

lives and writes in the woods near Maple, Wisconsin with her husband and crabby cat. Her chapbook *Target Practice* was published in 2009 by Parallel Press (University of Wisconsin Libraries). She currently serves as president of the Wisconsin Fellowship of Poets (wfop.org).

Ruth Z. Deming

writes from her home in Willow Grove, PA, a suburb of Philadelphia, in the good ole USA. Every morning, while her breakfast is cooling, she writes a poem and posts it on Facebook. Her work has been published in lit mags including *Creative Nonfiction*, *Mad Swirl*, *Literary Yard* and *Scarlet Leaf Review*. Before bed every night, she picks out one of the three or four books that are scattered on the "husband's side" of the bed to read herself to sleep. A psychotherapist, she runs New Directions Support Group for people with depression, bipolar disorder, and their loved ones. Her blog is www.ruthzdeming.blogspot.com.

Matt Dennison

spent after a rather extended and varied second childhood in New Orleans, and has had work appear in *Rattle*, *Bayou Magazine*, *Redivider*, *Natural Bridge*, *The Spoon River Poetry Review* and *Cider Press Review*, among others. He has also made short films with Michael Dickes, Swoon, and Marie Craven.

Nod Ghosh

works in a laboratory in Christchurch doing strange things with coloured light and body parts, whilst waiting for the next apocalypse. Nod has stories published in *Landfall*, *JAAM*, *Takahē* and various other New Zealand and overseas publications. Nod's story *The Cool Box* was runner up in the June 2017 Bath Flash Fiction award. For further details, please visit http://www.nodghosh.com/about/.

Jack Granath

is a library director in Kansas. His poetry has appeared in *Poetry East*, *Rattle*, and *North American Review* among other journals and magazines. His website is www.jackgranath.com.

John Grey

is an Australian-born, US-resident short story writer and poet. He has been published in numerous magazines including *Weird Tales*, *Christian Science Monitor*, *Greensboro Poetry Review*, *Agni*, *Poet Lore* and *Journal Of The American Medical Association* as well as the horror anthology *What Fears Become* and the science fiction anthology *Futuredaze*. He was the winner of the Rhysling Award for short genre poetry in 1999.

Louise Hofmeister

wrote lots of government grants and reports, then decided to pursue some more creative expression upon her recent retirement. She has Masters Degrees in Public Administration and the Psychology of Health Education, training she regularly overcomes. Still fairly new to writing poetry, she thoroughly enjoys exploring various forms and hanging out with marvelous teachers and poet-mentors including Les Bernstein and Judy Anderson.

Mark Hudson

lives in Evanston, Illinois, U.S.A, the closest northern suburb of Chicago. He spends most of his time creating either fiction, poetry, or art. He is getting to be a regular contributor to Matt Potter's Australian books, and other companies like to publish his work as well. His summer has been full of ups and downs, including ill family, bed bugs, canceled vacations, and other inconveniences. But he is most happy writing or creating art, even though it's always in his hometown. Whenever he happens to go out of town, which is rare, his creative imagination is sparked with ideas. He's sure Australia would be truly a paradise of inspiration!

Len Kuntz

is a writer from Washington State, an editor at the online magazine *Literary Orphans*. His latest story collection *At the Deep End* is forthcoming from Ravenna Press in 2018. You can also find more of his work here: lenkuntz.blogspot.com.

John Lambremont, Sr.

is a poet and writer from Baton Rouge, Louisiana, U.S.A. His poems have been published internationally in many reviews and anthologies, including *Pacific Review*, *The Minetta Review*, *Flint Hills Review*, and *Clarion*, and he has been nominated for The Pushcart Prize. John's full-length poetry volume, *The Moment*

Of Capture, was published in September 2017 by Lit Fest Press.

Larry Lefkowitz

has had stories, poetry, and humor widely published in journals, anthologies, and online. His literary novel, *The Novel, Kunzman, the Novel!* is available as an e-book and in print from Lulu.com and other distributors. Writers and readers with a deep interest in literature will especially enjoy the novel. His humorous fantasy and science fiction collection, *Laughing into the Fourth Dimension*, is available in print from Amazon books.

Cynthia Leslie-Bole

is a writing coach, editor and certified Amherst Writers and Artists Method group leader who has been published in *Pure Slush*, *Rootstalk* and *Moonshine Ink's Creative Brew*. Her collection of poetry, *The Luminous In-Between* (Azalea Arts Press, 2016), celebrates our innate capacity to create, heal, and perceive what lies beyond the ordinary. Cynthia lives in the San Francisco Bay Area. Find more at www.cynthialesliebole.com and www.theluminousinbetween.blogspot.com.

Michael Marrotti

is an author from Pittsburgh, using words instead of violence to mitigate the suffering of life in a callous world of redundancy. His primary goal is to help other people. He considers poetry to be a form of philanthropy. When he's not writing, he's volunteering at the Light Of Life homeless shelter on a weekly basis. If you appreciate the man's work, please check out his book, *F.D.A. Approved Poetry*, available at Amazon.

Todd McKie

is an artist and writer. He lurches from canvas to keyboard, bleary-eyed and paint-spattered, but grateful for the exercise. His stories have appeared in *PANK*, McSweeney's Internet Tendency, *STORY (Online)*, *Chicago Literati*, and elsewhere. Todd lives in Boston and he blogs at toddmckie.blogspot.com sporadically.

Lesley Middleton

retired from teaching and decided to resurrect her ambition to become a writer. Initially she thought freelance journalism might provide the challenge she was seeking but before long she realised: writing fiction is much more fun! She writes mostly short stories and flash fiction. Several of these have recently appeared in anthologies and two more are due to be published later in 2017.

Gwendolyn Joyce Mintz

is an award-winning writer and a photographer. Her work has appeared in various journals and she is the author of two chapbooks, *Mother Love* and *Where I'll Be If I'm Not There*. She blogs infrequently at http://wwwonewriter.blogspot.com.

Piet Nieuwland

worked on conservation management strategies for Te Papa Atawhai in New Zealand after training as a forester. His poems appear in journals including *Landfall*, *Brief*, *Catalyst*, *Takahe*, *Poetry NZ*, *Pure Slush*, *Mattoid*, *Blue Fifth Review* and most recently the NZ edition of *Atlanta Review*. He is a visual artist, edits *Fast Fibres Poetry*, reviews poetry for *Landfall Online Review* and lives near Whangarei.

Martin Jon Porter

is a teacher who lives in Melbourne. His most recent poetry has featured in *ArtAscent*, *Unusual Work* and *tamba*. His debut chapbook, *Traits*, was published by Ginninderra Press in 2016 as part of its Picaro Poets series.

Stephen V. Ramey

lives in beautiful New Castle, Pennsylvania, with his wife and two reformed feral cats. His work has appeared in many places, including The Journal of Compressed Creative Arts, The Doctor *T. J. Eckleburg Review*, and *Every Day Fiction*. His collection of (very) short fictions, *Glass Animals* (Pure Slush Books), is available wherever fine books are e-sold. For more information, go to www.stephenvramey.com, as well as facebook and twitter (@svramey).

Alex Robertson

enjoyed his formative years in Adelaide and spent his early working life around (country) South Australia and the Northern Territory. He has been published in university student publications and more recently in print and online journals. Since his location to the Adelaide Plains he has been involved in writing groups and broadcasting organisations around the north-eastern suburbs of Adelaide and Gawler.

Ruth Sabath Rosenthal

is a New York City poet, well published in the U.S.A. and, also, internationally. In October 2006, her poem 'on yet another birthday' was nominated for a Pushcart prize. Ruth's books are *Facing Home* (a chapbook); *Facing Home & beyond*; *little, but by no means small*; *Food: Nature vs Nurture*; and *Gone, but Not Easily Forgotten*. The books are available from Amazon.com. Find more of Ruth's work at her website and her blog site: http://newyorkcitypoet.com and http://poetrybyruthsabathrosenthal.com.

Wayne Scheer

has been nominated for four Pushcart Prizes and a Best of the Net. He's published numerous stories, poems and essays in print and online, including *Revealing Moments*, a collection of flash stories: https://issuu.com/pearnoir/docs/revealing_moments.
A short film was made of his short story, *Zen and the Art of House Painting*: https://vimeo.com/18491827.
Wayne lives with his wife in the U.S.

Martin Shaw

is fifty-two years old and has been writing for around ten years. Born in Luton, Bedfordshire, he then grew up in the Lincolnshire fens before moving to Cleethorpes. After being published in many online magazines, he now has his printed word appearing in the traditional paper press. He writes in the mornings and late evenings, and loves his family.

DL Shirey

writes from Portland, Oregon, USA, where it's probably raining. He has been caught flashing *at Café Aphra*, *365 Tomorrows*, *ZeroFlash*, *Fewer Than 500* and others listed at www.dlshirey.com.

Jan Elman Stout

has had fiction published in *Pure Slush*, *Literary Orphans*, *Journal of Compressed Creative Arts*, *Midwestern Gothic*, *Shotgun Honey*, *The Airgonaut*, *Jellyfish Review*, *(b)OINK* and elsewhere. She is a reader for *SmokeLong Quarterly*. In her former life she was a psychologist. Jan lives with her husband in Washington, DC.

Sophie Van Llewyn

lives in Germany. Her work has appeared in the 2017 *NFFD Anthology*, *New Delta Review*, *Hermeneutic Chaos Journal*, among others, and has been nominated for a Pushcart Prize. She is now currently at work on an historical novel. You can find out more about her at https://sophievanllewyn.wordpress.com.

Jerry Vilhotti

has had two collections of works published. The first, *Gods Depicting Pastime*, has the Greek gods discovering a game once played by people – who plastered their bodies with empire blue to be one with the sky, and tried to figure out what the tic infested thing was all about. The second collection, *Specs in the Eyes of Seeing*, follows a little boy's long journey from childhood to manhood.

Rob Walker

rob walker (n)

pron./rob wȯkə /

1. a cantankerous curmudgeon with a titanium knee

2. an original cliché

3. www.robwalkerpoet.com

Mercedes Webb-Pullman

gained an MA in Creative Writing through the International Institute of Modern Letters (IIML) at Victoria University, Wellington, in 2011. Her work has appeared online and in print in New Zealand, Australia, Canada, USA, UK, Ireland, Spain, and Palestine, in *Turbine*, *4th Floor*, *Pure Slush*, *Swamp*, *Scum*, *Reconfigurations*, *The Electronic Bridge*, *Otoliths*, *Connotations*, *The Red Room Company*, *riverbabble*, *Kind of a Hurricane Press*, and *Caesura*, among others, and in her books. She lives in Paekakariki, New Zealand.

Allan J. Wills

learned from standing in his children's shoes that his own experience of the world and the biases and prejudices that had produced was something akin to watching a black and white episode of *Dr Who* on a 1970s TV with a very snowy screen and maladjusted horizontal hold.

About the Artist

Damasque Wells

was born in Semaphore, South Australia. Attending art school in the late 1990s, Damasque dabbled in all things creative including ceramics, printmaking, photography, drawing and sculpture, among others.

Continuing to experiment in all mediums, Damasque is currently studying Jewellery and Object Design, exploring her love of culture, colour, pattern and texture, developing a new sense of creative self-expression, and unearthing a unique creative methodology.

Damasque's original artwork *Man with a Blue Rinse* (opposite) not only features on the front cover of this anthology, but inspired its theme.

Track Tales
by Mercedes Webb–Pullman

978-1-925536-35-5 (paperback)
978-1-925536-36-2 (eBook)

Mercedes Webb-Pullman illustrates her characters with a deft hand, sparing no feelings, laying herself and her world bare. Crime and corruption fade into a background of misogyny, deceit and human detritus "A thousand cockroaches deep". This is an outstanding, cohesive collection of impeccably-crafted poetry from the hand of a poet whose voice is ever-changing but always challenging, authentic and exciting.

Luck and Other Truths
by Richard Mark Glover

978-1-925101-77-5 (paperback)
978-1-925536-04-1 (eBook)

Richard Mark Glover spins larger-than-life tales of folks on the fringe in places where they tend to collect, with the focus on that great empty space known as Far West Texas. What might appear to outsiders as a whole bunch of harsh forbidding nothing – think Cormac McCarthy – these stories are filled with quirky characters brought to life by Glover's observant eye and quirk-spotting pen.

True Truth Serum Vol. #1

978-1-925536-29-4 (paperback)
978-1-925536-30-0 (eBook)

Stories, essays and poetry by Mercedes Webb-Pullman, Mark Hudson, Lynn Hoffman, Len Kuntz, Danielle Davis, M. Earl Smith, Wayne Scheer, Sally Reno, Vivian Wagner, Paul Beckman, Michael Konik, David S. Atkinson, A J Huffman, Jack Granath, Tim Philippart, Martin Jon Porter, Martin Shaw, Sylvia Aguilar-Zéleny, Ruth Z. Deming, John Lambremont, Sr., John Grey, Em König, Brian Abiri-Osare, Patricia Walsh, Samuel Cole, Danny P. Barbare, Carl 'Papa' Palmer, Michael Marrotti, Barbara Ruth, Stephen V. Ramey, Ruth Sabath Rosenthal, Irene Buckler, Robbi Nester, Flora Gaugg, Matt Devirgiliis, Sarah Anne Childers, Robert Beveridge, Anne E. Weisgerber, Richard King Perkins II, Nod Ghosh, Alan Walowitz, Tom Sheehan, Dusty-Anne Rhodes, Lynn White and Gwendolyn Joyce Mintz.

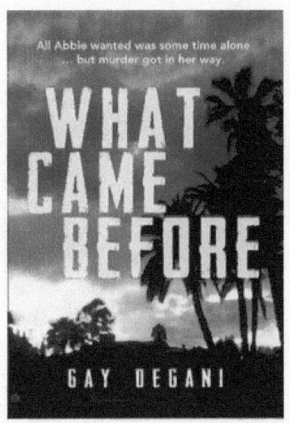

Based on True Stories
by Matt Potter

978-1-925101-75-1 (paperback)
978-1-925101-76-8 (eBook)

The small fictions in *Based on True Stories* will not lull you —
they will piss you off or, at the least, move you to indignation,
or tears, or laughter. Maybe all three. These gems provoke, like
the tip of a chef's knife pricking skin, and just as the words get
uncomfortable, the story delivers the bit of redemption that
reveals the humanity of his characters — and of us all. These
stories are real, raw, and honest. The reading doesn't get much
better than that.

Also from Truth Serum Press
http://truthserumpress.net/catalogue/

happyme@t.us
by Kim Conklin

978-1-925536-07-2 (paperback)
978-1-925536-08-9 (eBook)

To be everywhere and nowhere, all at once … Through her stories, Kim Conklin takes us on a journey of the human condition, where the everyday becomes foreign and dangerous, while the oddities of our world provide us with strange comfort. Each story is unsettling, passionate, thoughtful, provocative and reaffirming; taking the reader everywhere and nowhere, all at once. Dark tales, deftly told.